Karen's Yo-Yo

Little Sister

Karen's Yo-Yo

Ann M. Martin

Illustrations by Susan Crocca Tang

A
LITTLE APPLE
PAPERBACK

SCHOLASTIC INC.
New York Toronto London Auckland Sydney
Mexico City New Delhi Hong Kong

*The author gratefully acknowledges
Gabrielle Charbonnet
for her help
with this book.*

ISBN 0-590-52511-5

12 11 10 9 8 7 6 5 4 3 2 1   0 1 2 3 4 5/0

Printed in the U.S.A.   40
First Scholastic printing, March 2000

Team Yo!

"Grab your coat," called Daddy. He was standing by the front door. "Andrew and I are leaving now."

Daddy, my little brother, Andrew, and I were going to walk downtown to buy new spring jackets. It was a Friday afternoon in March, and the weather was just beginning to warm up a little. (Usually Daddy would be working on a Friday afternoon. But he did not want to miss the first warm day of the year, so he took the afternoon off.)

"I am coming!" I yelled. I pulled on my

winter coat (it was almost too small for me) and raced to the door.

"My new jacket is going to have racing stripes," said Andrew as we walked down the sidewalk. "Vrrrrroom! Racing stripes will help me run fast."

Andrew started running.

"Hey, wait up!" I said. I ran after him. Since I am older and have longer legs, I caught up to him quickly.

I will tell you about Andrew and the rest of my family soon. But for now it is enough to say that I am seven and Andrew is four going on five.

We came to the corner.

"We have to wait for Daddy," said Andrew.

We did not have to wait. Only Andrew had to. Fours are not allowed to cross the street by themselves. Sevens are allowed, if they look carefully both ways. But I decided to be a nice big sister and wait with Andrew for Daddy.

"I am thinking of getting a turquoise

jacket," I said. "Or maybe teal." (Turquoise and teal are fancy shades of blue.)

"Oh," said Andrew.

"Those are kinds of blue," I explained.

"Oh," he said again.

Daddy reached the corner and took our hands, and we crossed.

It did not take very long to walk downtown. Once we were there, Daddy, Andrew, and I headed for Bellair's Department Store. Bellair's is huge and sells everything. I love Bellair's, and I was eager to start shopping.

But before we arrived at Bellair's, we noticed a crowd of people in the little park in front of Stoneybrook Town Hall. (Stoneybrook is the name of the town in Connecticut where I live. But more about that later.) The people were cheering and applauding.

"Come on, Daddy. Come on, Andrew," I said. "I want to see what those people are cheering about."

I raced to the crowd and wormed my way through it. I am a very skillful crowd-wormer. It helps to be small.

3

Well, I could not believe my eyes. Performing in front of all those people were four teenagers. They were doing the coolest, most gigundoly fantastic tricks with — yo-yos!

One boy made his yo-yo fly around and around in a big circle. A girl made hers skitter across the ground. Two other boys were shooting their yo-yos toward each other as if they were fighting, but the yo-yos never touched. The four yo-yoers wore shiny black-and-pink satin jackets with bright patches all the way up the sleeves. The patches looked so, so cool. On the backs of the jackets, in bright pink script, was written TEAM YO!

The four yo-yoers finished up their routine with an amazing, fancy trick that was so complicated I cannot even describe it.

I yelled and whistled and clapped along with everyone else.

Then one of the yo-yo boys announced a contest (I love contests!), and several kids not much older than me stepped out of the

4

crowd. The members of Team Yo! explained that these kids were going to compete for patches just like the ones on the Team Yo! jackets.

Wow! Did I want one of those yo-yo patches too!

Suddenly I decided two things: 1) My new jacket was going to be black and pink (not teal), and 2) I needed a yo-yo, right away.

Two of Everything

Guess what? We never made it to Bellair's that day. Andrew and Daddy and I watched Team Yo! do tricks for so long that, by the time we were ready to leave, it was suppertime. So we walked back to the big house.

Oh! I have not told you yet about the big house and the little house and my two families. You are probably dying to know everything, so I will tell you.

Let me start at the beginning.

A long, long time ago, when I was small, I

lived in the big house here in Stoneybrook with my mommy and daddy and Andrew.

Then Mommy and Daddy started arguing. They tried to work things out, but they could not do it. They told Andrew and me that they loved us very much. But they did not want to be married to each other anymore. So they got divorced.

Mommy moved out with Andrew and me to a little house not far away. Soon she met a nice man named Seth Engle. She and Seth got married, and that is how Seth became my stepfather.

Now at the little house live Mommy, Seth, Andrew, me — and some pets. They are Emily Junior, my rat; Bob, Andrew's hermit crab; Midgie, Seth's dog; and Rocky, Seth's cat.

Daddy stayed in the big house after he and Mommy got divorced. (It is the house he grew up in.) He met a woman named Elizabeth Thomas, and they got married. Elizabeth is my stepmother. She is not the evil-stepmother kind, like Cinderella's. She is a very nice stepmother.

Elizabeth was married once before and has four children of her own. They are David Michael, who is seven like me; Kristy, who is thirteen and the best stepsister ever; and Sam and Charlie, who are in high school and are practically grown-ups (though sometimes they are as silly as kindergartners).

Then Daddy and Elizabeth adopted my sister Emily Michelle from the faraway country of Vietnam. She is two and a half. I love her so much that I named my rat after her.

Nannie, who is Elizabeth's mother, came to live at the big house to help with Emily Michelle. Actually, Nannie helps with everybody!

Now for the names of the big-house pets: They are Shannon, David Michael's big Bernese mountain dog puppy; Pumpkin, our kitten; Crystal Light the Second, my goldfish; and Goldfishie, Andrew's you-know-what.

Nowadays, so that Andrew and I can spend equal amounts of time with both our mommy and our daddy, we switch houses almost every month. We spend one month at the big house with our big-house family, then one month at the little house with our little-house family.

Because we have two houses, two mommies, two daddies, and two of a bunch of other things, I gave Andrew and me special names. I call us Andrew Two-Two and Karen Two-Two. (I thought up those names after my teacher read a book to our class. It was called *Jacob Two-Two Meets the Hooded Fang*.) We have two sets of toys and clothes and books. We have two bicycles, one at each house. I have two stuffed cats. Moosie lives at the big house. Goosie lives at the little house. And I wear two pairs of glasses. (Not at the same time!) Pink ones for most of the time and blue ones for reading up close.

10

I also have two best friends: Hannie Papadakis lives across the street and one house over from the big house. Nancy Dawes lives next door to the little house. We spend so much time together that we call ourselves the Three Musketeers. Our motto is "All for one, and one for all!" The three of us are in the same class at school.

Sometimes being a two-two is complicated. But usually it is pretty great. And I just noticed something. What is the perfect toy for a two-two?

I will give you a hint. It starts with "yo" and ends with "yo." You guessed it: a yo-yo!

A yo-yo for a two-two. Perfect!

The Genius

"Yo-yos for two-twos! Two-twos for yo-yos!" Andrew and I marched around the kitchen table, chanting. "Yo-yos for two-twos! Two-twos for yo-yos!"

It was Saturday afternoon. On the kitchen table lay a pile of crumpled dollar bills, a few quarters, some dimes and nickels, and many, many pennies. Andrew and I had pooled our savings. Most of the dollar bills, quarters, and dimes were mine. Andrew had mostly pennies. I had decided to share equally with Andrew, though. (I am a generous big sister.) Guess what? There was enough money for two yo-yos!

"After we go to Toy City for yo-yos, we still need to go to Bellair's for jackets," Daddy reminded us.

"Yea!" we yelled. "Toy City! Toy City! We love Toy City!"

This time we drove. (Daddy wanted to make sure we actually got to Bellair's.)

Toy City is the most gigundoly fabulous toy store. It is huge. Really huge. It has every toy you could possibly think of. It has a whole aisle of dolls. A whole aisle of little cars. A whole aisle of tea sets and kitchen sets. Sometimes I wish Daddy would accidentally forget me at Toy City and I could spend the night there, playing with all the toys. I would not mind. Well, maybe it would be better if Hannie and Nancy were with me.

Guess what else Toy City had a whole aisle of? Yes! Yo-yos! You would not believe how many different yo-yos Toy City had. I saw yo-yos in every color of the rainbow.

Glow-in-the-dark ones. Ones that shot out sparks. Yo-yos that would automatically come back up the string. Yo-yos that would automatically stay at the bottom of the string. Yo-yos shaped like hearts, four-leaf clovers, stars, and diamonds. There were so many to choose from!

Finally a clerk walked up the aisle. "May I help you?" he asked.

"You certainly may," I said, very importantly. (I love being waited on in stores.) "My little brother and I are trying to choose yo-yos, but there are so many. We do not know which ones to buy."

The clerk explained the differences among some of the yo-yos. He recommended a small one for Andrew. "It will fit your hand better," the clerk said.

"Thank you," said Andrew. He chose a small blue one.

"Which one is the best for doing tricks?" I asked.

"Can you do yo-yo tricks?" said the clerk.

"No, but soon I will be able to," I said confidently.

The clerk reached up to the top shelf and took down a yo-yo in an oversized box.

"This is the Genius," said the clerk, handing me the box. I stared at the Genius through the plastic. It was round (not clover-shaped or anything) and made of gleaming silver metal. It looked like a spaceship.

"It is beautiful," I said softly.

"It is the last one in the store," the clerk told me. "The Genius is famous for its perfect balance and superb string action. And," he added, turning the box over, "the Genius comes with its own instructional video."

My eyes opened wide. An instructional video! I read the box cover. In big letters were the words THE GENIUS—YO-YO OF CHAMPIONS! In slightly smaller letters was written, Official Yo-Yo of Team Yo!

Well! Not only was the Genius beautiful and shiny and silver, it came with its own

video and was recommended by Team Yo! It was definitely the yo-yo for Karen Brewer, future yo-yo champion!

"I will take it," I said.

Andrew's yo-yo cost two dollars and forty-nine cents. The Genius cost much, much more. I emptied out my pockets on the Toy City counter and carefully smoothed out my dollar bills. I made stacks with my quarters and dimes and nickels. In the end, I still had to borrow two dollars from Daddy. But it was worth it. After all, I was getting an instructional video too.

Daddy said we could not play with our yo-yos until after we had bought new jackets at Bellair's.

You have probably never seen two kids pick out jackets as quickly as Andrew and I did that day.

Andrew ran into the boys' department and grabbed a maroon polar-fleece warm-up jacket. It was the first one he saw. "This one!" he said. "This is fine!" (He had forgotten about his racing stripes.) Daddy helped him find one in his size.

In the girls' department, I forced myself to look around a little. I did not want to end up with a plain maroon jacket. I discovered that Bellair's did not have any black-and-pink jackets at all. So I would not look like a Team Yo! member. Boo and bullfrogs. However, I did find a cute pink-and-green jacket. It had a hood and pockets big enough to hold my Genius. "This one is okay," I said.

"Are you sure?" asked Daddy.

"Yes." I did not really care about my new jacket. I was just glad my beautiful new yo-yo could fit into the pockets of the jacket.

I planned on taking the Genius with me everywhere.

Walking the Dog

That night Andrew and I watched *The Genius: Mastering the Art of the Yo-Yo*. We saw different people doing amazing things with their own Genius yo-yos. I was very excited, knowing that soon I would be able to do those things too.

But I learned there was a lot I had to do before I could even begin yo-yoing. First I had to cut the string of my yo-yo to the right height. It could not be too long, because it would bump the floor when I spun it. It could not be too short, because I would not be able to do certain tricks if it were.

A yo-yo string is the perfect length when the yo-yo is resting on the floor and the end of the string is at your belly button. I had to cut three inches off the Genius's string. Then I had to put a slip knot at the end of the string. (Daddy tied it for me. He tied Andrew's too. Andrew had to cut eight inches off his string.) The slip knot went around my middle finger — not my pointer finger, as I had thought. Then the string had to be wound around the yo-yo. This was hard at first because it kept slipping around the yo-yo's middle, which the video called the axle. But I finally got it.

Well, when all that was done, I had seen the first part of *Mastering the Art of the Yo-Yo* seven times and it was time for bed. At first, Andrew had watched the video with me and tried to do everything I did. But after a while he left. He said as long as his yo-yo went up and down, that was good enough for him. That's the difference between a four-year-old and a seven-year-old.

Early on Sunday morning I leaped out of bed and grabbed the Genius from my dresser. I was ready to start yo-yoing.

The first skill to master, when learning the art of the yo-yo, is making your yo-yo "sleep." First you tuck it in tightly and kiss it good-night. Just kidding! Making your yo-yo sleep just means that it spins really fast at the end of the string, without coming up. It looks pretty hard, but it is really not difficult to do.

All you do is hold your yo-yo in your hand, palm up, and flick your wrist down in a sharp movement. The yo-yo flies down to the end of the string, and if you are a yo-yo genius and your yo-yo is a Genius, it stays there. Then you flick your hand up a little bit, and the yo-yo will come back up the string into your hand.

I practiced putting my yo-yo to sleep for about half an hour before breakfast. Sometimes I did not flick the Genius down straight enough, and it spun out of control. When it did that, there was no way to get it to come back up again. I had to grab it and wind it back up by hand. But soon I was making the Genius sleep almost every time, and I hardly ever had to stop and wind it back up. I was a natural.

After breakfast I popped *Mastering the Art of the Yo-Yo* back in the VCR and watched the members of Team Yo! demonstrate the first trick. It was called Walk the Dog. What you do is this: You make the yo-yo sleep at the end of the string. Then you gently lower your hand until the yo-yo touches the floor. The yo-yo will skitter across the floor like a dog walking. Then you flick the yo-yo back up. Simple.

I watched the Team Yo!-yoers walk the dog five or six times. Then I tried it myself. I did it on the first try. Yea!

The second and third times I tried it, the Genius went out of control. But that did not matter. I had done my first real trick. Soon I would be a yo-yo master.

I was very, very excited. I watched *Mastering the Art of the Yo-Yo* all the way through to the end. There were lots and lots more tricks to learn. Some looked really hard. I would have to learn those later.

At the end of the video was the very best part — a Team Yo! girl explained that Team Yo! did demonstrations all over the country, in which kids could win patches and other prizes for doing tricks. There was even information on how to enter the national championship.

Now, I could not really see myself as the yo-yoing national champion. But I knew I could learn enough tricks to win some patches for my new jacket. I imagined myself wearing my patched jacket to school. Everyone would be so impressed!

Now I could not wait for Team Yo! to return to Stoneybrook. I wondered when that would be.

The Substitute

On Monday I wore my green-and-pink jacket, with my yo-yo in the pocket, to school. I was happy to be back in my second-grade class with the other Two Musketeers. Everyone else in class was eager to talk about yo-yos too. A lot of us had seen Team Yo! performing in Stoneybrook. Yoyos were the latest craze, as Daddy put it. Just last week, there were no yo-yos around. Now they were everywhere. And I had a Genius.

I love school.

The bell rang. I ran for my seat and put the Genius in my desk. I was looking forward to seeing Ms. Colman, who is the best teacher in the world. And in walked a teacher — but it was not Ms. Colman! Suddenly I remembered that Ms. Colman had told us she would be away this week.

The new teacher looked at us. She did not smile. In my opinion, teachers should smile a lot. Ms. Colman does.

"Class, my name is Ms. Holland," said the teacher. "I will be your substitute teacher until Ms. Colman returns from her conference."

Kids started whispering to one another. Everyone had forgotten that Ms. Colman was going to be away.

"Class!" Ms. Holland said, clapping her hands sharply. "Quiet, please. And young lady" — she pointed at Natalie Springer — "deposit that gum in the wastepaper basket. There will be no gum chewing in this classroom."

Natalie hurried to the wastebasket and

threw her gum away. When she returned to her seat, her face was red. She had been embarrassed by the substitute.

I had a feeling I was not going to like Ms. Holland very much. But Ms. Colman had asked us to behave while she was gone, so I told myself to be good.

"Now I will take attendance," said Ms. Holland. "Tammy Barkan?"

"Here," said Tammy.

I raised my hand. "Um, Ms. Holland?" I said. "Ms. Colman does not take attendance herself. She lets one of us do it."

Ms. Holland looked at me for a moment. Then she said, "And what is your name, may I ask?"

"Karen Brewer," I said.

"Well, Karen, Ms. Colman is not here today. I am. And when I teach class, I take attendance. Is that clear?"

I nodded. "Yes," I said. It was clear. It was clear that Ms. Holland was no Ms. Colman.

Recess

The rest of the morning did not go as badly as the first few minutes. Ms. Holland read aloud from the newspaper. (Borrrring!) Then we did writing exercises. Then it was time for recess. Yea!

I made sure to take the Genius out of my desk and stash it in my jacket pocket on the way outside.

On the playground, I pulled the Genius out to show Hannie and Nancy some simple up-and-down movements.

"Wow," said Hannie.

"I cannot believe how good you already are," said Nancy.

I smiled at them. "I will teach you both everything I know," I said. "Because we are best friends."

"Cool yo-yo," said Ricky Torres, my pretend husband. (We had once had a wedding on that very spot of the playground.)

"Thanks," I said proudly. "It is called the Genius. Watch this. I can Walk the Dog."

I flicked the yo-yo down, and it skittered across the blacktop.

"Wow!" said Bobby Giannelli. "That was great."

Bobby had a yo-yo too. (It was not nearly as fancy as the Genius.) He flicked it up and down a few times. He could get it to sleep for a moment or two, but not long enough to Walk the Dog.

"I wish I had a cool yo-yo like yours," Bobby said.

"It does help with tricks to have a top-of-the-line model like the Genius," I said. "But there are no more at Toy City. I bought the last one. Maybe you could find one somewhere else," I added. I did not want to make Bobby feel bad that his yo-yo was not as good as mine, even though it was true.

"Maybe," Bobby said sadly.

Just then Pamela Harding, my best enemy, joined us.

"Cool yo-yo," said Pamela. "It is almost as cool as mine, the Spin Wizard."

Pamela held out the Spin Wizard. It was emerald green, with specks of gold. I had to admit it was pretty cool looking — almost as cool as the Genius.

"Watch me go Around the World," said Pamela. She threw her yo-yo out underhanded, flung it around in a big circle, and snapped it back to her hand.

"Wow!" Ricky, Bobby, Hannie, Nancy, and I shouted.

"Now watch me Loop the Loop," said Pamela. This time she flicked the yo-yo down, swung it up in a big loop, sent it down again, and then snapped it back up.

"Cool!" we exclaimed. By now three or four other kids, all with yo-yos, were crowded around watching Pamela do tricks.

Pamela grinned. "All it takes is a little practice," she said modestly.

My mouth dropped open. Pamela Harding, modest? This was something new and surprising.

Then something else new and surprising happened. Leslie Morris, Pamela's best friend and my second-best enemy, actually said to me, "Karen, I heard you saying that you saw Team Yo! perform. I did too. They were great!"

First Pamela acting modest, and now Leslie being friendly with me. Yo-yoing really brings out the best in people, I said to myself.

"Yes, I thought Team Yo! was fantastic," I said to Leslie.

"I hear they even come to schools," said

Leslie. "They teach science with yo-yos. I hope they come to Stoneybrook Academy sometime." (That is the name of my school, in case I have forgotten to tell you.)

"Me too," I said. "That would be awesome!"

The Pendulum

"Time for science," said Ms. Holland after lunch. "Today we are studying pendulums. Does anyone know what a pendulum is?"

Ian Johnson raised his hand. "A pendulum is something that swings back and forth."

"Very good," said Ms. Holland. "Now we are going to read aloud from our science books about pendulums. I would like the class to divide into groups of three. Students will take turns reading aloud to one another."

My group was Hannie (yea!), Hank Reubens, and I. We took turns reading from the science book.

When my turn came, I read a very long paragraph. It was hard to understand.

"I do not get it," Hank interrupted.

"Me neither," said Hannie.

"Hmm," I said. "I am not sure I get it either. It sounds like the book is trying to say that a long pendulum swings slowly and a short pendulum swings quickly."

"Maybe," said Hank. "But I am not sure."

"I have an idea," I said. I reached into my desk and brought out the Genius. "We can do an experiment." I lowered the Genius a little way down the string and let it swing back and forth. "It is swinging very quickly, like a short pendulum," I observed. Then I let the Genius roll down to the end of the string and swung it gently. "Now that it is a long pendulum, it swings more slowly."

"Hey," said Hannie. "That is great. Now I get it."

"Me too," said Hank.

I smiled. "And all thanks to the Gen — "

"What is that toy doing out, young lady?" snapped a loud, angry voice.

I whirled around. Ms. Holland was standing behind me, with her hands on her hips. "It is my yo-yo. I was just — " I began.

"I can see that it is a yo-yo, and I can see that you are using valuable class time to play with toys." Ms. Holland held out her hand. "Give it to me."

I started to argue. "But I was just showing how a pendu — "

"You were just playing," Ms. Holland interrupted. "Now hand it over."

This was so unfair! But what could I do? I gave the substitute my yo-yo. She put it in a drawer in Ms. Colman's desk.

"Now," Ms. Holland said, slamming the desk drawer shut. "Does anyone else have a toy they need me to hold for them? No? Then it is time for spelling."

I was so upset my teeth hurt.

When the last bell rang at the end of the day, I walked up to Ms. Holland.

"May I have my yo-yo back, please?" I asked politely. The class rule is that toys that are taken away during class are returned the next day. But since my toy had been taken from me unfairly, I figured Ms. Holland should return it to me early.

"I am afraid not," said Ms. Holland. "I will leave it to Ms. Colman to decide when you get your yo-yo back."

I guessed that Ms. Holland would call Ms. Colman at her conference that night. Then she would find out what the class rule was.

So I would have to wait until the next day after all. Ms. Holland was sure to give me back the Genius then.

"Well, okay," I said. "See you tomorrow." I turned and left.

Counting to Four Hundred

Ms. Holland had been very angry at me over the yo-yo on Monday. I did not want her not to like me for almost a whole week. I cannot stand it when someone does not like me even for a day. (Except Pamela Harding. That does not bother me too much.)

So on Tuesday I decided to start being the perfect student. I would not even mention getting back the Genius first thing in the morning. I would try to wait until Ms. Holland offered it to me, probably after lunch.

That is when Ms. Colman usually returns toys that have been taken away.

If I was as good as gold all week, by Friday Ms. Holland would love me.

During geography class, I raised my hand every time Ms. Holland asked a question. (I am a quick map-reader.) I also raised my hand all through social studies.

During art I did not spill my glue or get paint on my shoes. I drew a beautiful cat that looked like what Pumpkin, the big-house kitten, would look like if Pumpkin were green and purple instead of black. Ms. Holland said it was very nice.

I had told myself I would not ask Ms. Holland for the Genius, but by the time lunch had ended, I was going crazy. There were lots of reasons why. 1) Ms. Holland should not have taken the Genius in the first place. 2) I had not played with the Genius all yesterday evening at home. 3) I had not played with the Genius this morning before school. 4) I had not played with the Genius during morning recess. 5) I had not played with the Genius during lunch. 6) My friends all had their yo-yos and were playing with them right in front of me.

So after lunch, I could not wait any longer. I stood by Ms. Holland, who was sitting at Ms. Colman's desk.

"May I have my yo-yo back now, please?" I asked.

Ms. Holland raised her eyebrows. "I told you already, Karen. I will let Ms. Colman decide when you get your toy back."

"Oh, was Ms. Colman out when you called last night?" I said, smiling. "That is bad luck. But I can tell you what she would have said. The class rule is that toys are returned the next day." I held out my hand. "I would like my yo-yo, please."

Ms. Holland looked at my hand as if it were a disgusting slug.

"I do not think you understand, young lady," Ms. Holland said. "I am not going to bother Ms. Colman at her conference. Your toy will be in her desk waiting for her when she returns next week. She may or may not choose to return it to you then. In the meantime, I do not want to hear another word about — "

"But it is the class rule!" I wailed. I was almost crying, I was so frustrated.

"When I am the teacher, it is my class, and I make the rules," Ms. Holland said in a mean voice. "Now take your seat. Class is about to begin."

Boy, was I angry. It was so, so unfair! Ms. Holland should not have taken the Genius from me in the first place. And now, on top of that, she was breaking the class rule and not giving it back to me.

I hardly heard a word that was said all through phonics and math and silent reading. Okay, not much was said during silent reading. But if anyone had said anything, I would not have heard it. I was too mad.

Mommy tells me to count to ten when I

feel like I am about to lose my temper. Well, that afternoon I counted past four hundred before I began to feel okay again.

I reminded myself that I still had almost a whole week to go with the substitute. It was not too late to get back on her good side. Maybe, if I won Ms. Holland over and proved to her what a great kid I really am, she would change her mind and give me the Genius back early.

Four hundred twelve, four hundred thirteen, four hundred fourteen, I counted silently to myself. I was not angry any longer. I was determined once again to be the perfect student.

Ms. Holland was writing at the blackboard. She was drawing some kind of square or rectangle. (I had not been paying attention, so I do not know what she was trying to teach us.)

"I need colored chalk for this diagram," she said. "Class, does anyone know where Ms. Colman keeps the colored chalk?"

I raised my hand. "I do," I said. "I will get it for you."

"Thank you, Karen," said Ms. Holland.

I opened the drawer in Ms. Colman's desk where she keeps chalk, glue, staples, and other fun supplies.

There was the Genius, right next to a stack of construction paper! In the back of the drawer was a box of colored chalk.

I reached into the back of the drawer with my right hand to grab the chalk. Somehow my left hand fell on the Genius. My fingers curled around it. As if it had a mind of its own, my left hand slipped the Genius into the waistband of my jeans and smoothed my sweater over it. I could not believe it.

I shut the drawer, walked to Ms. Holland, handed her the chalk, and returned to my desk. My face was burning, but I felt happy.

The Genius was mine again, just the way it should have been all along.

Cuckoo for Yo-yos

I was very, very careful the next morning to make sure Ms. Holland was not on the playground when I took out the Genius. I had played with it all the night before at home. I had been *very* glad to have it back. I did not really want to think about *how* I had gotten it back. I just wanted to practice, practice, practice.

"I see Ms. Holland gave you your yo-yo back," said Hannie. "I am glad she stuck to the class rule. Not all substitutes would, you know."

"Um, yes, I know," I said. For some reason I did not want to tell Hannie what I had done. "Anyway, I am glad to have my yo-yo back."

I was sure Ms. Holland would never even notice the Genius was gone. She was probably sure it was gathering dust at the back of Ms. Colman's desk drawer. But I did not want her to see that I had it, just in case.

Hannie and Nancy had now gotten new yo-yos of their own. I was glad we could practice together. Hannie's was purple with a gold rim and was called the Magician. Nancy's yo-yo had swirls of yellow and orange and teal (that is a kind of blue, remember?) and was called the Spin Doctor.

"Those are both great," I told my friends.

They showed me the tricks they could do. Hannie could Rock the Baby. Nancy did a Lunar Loop. I was impressed.

"Watch this!" called Pamela. "It is called Johnny Round the Corner."

A bunch of kids gathered around Pamela to watch her do her trick. She flipped her yo-yo down into a sleeper. Then she put her right hand over her shoulder, as if she were throwing a ball. She flicked the yo-yo up, and it shot over her hand and down again. Then she pulled it up one more time and caught it. It was a great trick.

"Cool!" we cried.

"Watch how long I can make my new yo-yo sleep," said Bobby. He flicked his yo-yo down and started counting slowly. He got to twenty-eight before he twitched the yo-yo back up the string. "My record is thirty-seven," he said.

Wow. That was a long time. I had not even tried to see how long I could get the Genius to sleep. I wondered if I could beat Bobby's record.

Everyone in my class had gone cuckoo for yo-yos. My friends were doing fancy tricks. But all I could do was Walk the Dog. And I was not even the best one at that. Addie Sidney could Walk the Dog and make it look like her yo-yo was pulling her along in her wheelchair.

I had lost valuable practice time while the Genius was in Ms. Colman's desk. I would have to study the rest of *Mastering the Art of the Yo-Yo* tonight and start learning some fancy new tricks quickly, if I wanted to keep up.

"It would be fun to see who in our class knows the most yo-yo tricks," I said to Hannie and Nancy.

"Yes. And who is the best at doing them," said Nancy.

"That would be fun," said Hannie. "But who could we get to judge? I do not think Ms. Colman knows enough about yo-yoing to say who is best."

Suddenly I had an idea. "Hey!" I said. "Leslie said that Team Yo! sometimes visits schools. Maybe they could come to Stoneybrook Academy and judge a competition! Kids could compete for patches and other prizes, and maybe there could be a school champion."

"That is a terrific idea, Karen!" said Nancy.

"Yeah, I think we should tell the other kids," said Hannie.

And so we did. All my classmates thought my idea was great too. (Leslie said something about Team Yo! visiting schools to teach science, not to judge competitions. But we did not pay much attention to her.)

We were more cuckoo for yo-yos than ever.

Rock the Baby

That morning during class, I did not touch my Genius once, not even to make sure it was still in my desk. And every time Ms. Holland opened Ms. Colman's desk, I held my breath. But she did not seem to notice the Genius was gone. I tried to convince myself that she had forgotten about it. But I am not sure I believed myself.

After lunchtime, out on the playground again, all the kids (except me) took out their yo-yos. I did not take the Genius out of my jacket pocket. I had seen Ms. Holland walking through the playground on her way to the teachers' lounge. I could not take any chances.

"I can do Around the World now," said Bobby. He threw his yo-yo out underhand, whirled it around in a big circle, and caught it.

It looked like one of the easier tricks, much easier than Pamela's Johnny Round the Corner, for instance. I knew I would be able to do it, and I was dying to try. But still I did not take the Genius out of my jacket pocket. I had to be strong.

Then Hannie showed us Rock the Baby again.

"That is really neat," said Bobby. "Will you show me how to do it?"

"Sure," said Hannie. "Karen, do you know how to Rock the Baby?"

I shook my head no. This was killing me.

"Why don't you get out your yo-yo and I will teach you too?" said Hannie.

I glanced around. Ms. Holland was at the edge of the blacktop. "Um, I will just watch instead."

"Okay," said Hannie. Then she showed Bobby and me how to Rock the Baby.

First she put her yo-yo into a sleeper. Then she reached down with her left hand and grasped the string about halfway down. With her right hand she pinched the string again, halfway between her left hand and the yo-yo. Then with her left hand she made a little triangle of string, for a cradle, beneath the yo-yo. And finally she rocked the "baby" (the yo-yo, really) in the cradle. When she was done, she let go of the string all at once, the yo-yo fell, and then zipped back up to her hand.

"Ta-daa!" said Hannie. "Linny taught me that." Linny is Hannie's big brother. He is nine.

"Wow — so cool," I said. My fingers were itching to try it.

Hannie had to show Bobby three or four times where to put his hands, how to grab the string, and so on. But Bobby was getting it, slowly.

I really, really, really, *really* wanted to try

Rocking the Baby too. I could not stand it.

I looked around. I did not see Ms. Holland anywhere.

I took the Genius out of my pocket, slipped the string onto my finger, and flipped it down into a sleeper.

"Now, where do I grab the string?" I asked Hannie.

Hannie said, "About halfway — "

"Karen Brewer!" said a loud voice behind me. "What are you doing with that yo-yo?"

I turned and felt the blood rush to my face. Ms. Holland was staring at me with her arms crossed.

"I — I — I — " I tried to say. But no explanation came out. The Genius spun out of control and flopped over on the ground on its side.

"Hand it over this instant," said Ms. Holland. "And I will see you after class. We need to have a talk, young lady."

I had a feeling it was not going to be a very pleasant talk.

Talking to Ms. Holland

Well. You can imagine how awful that afternoon was. Hannie and Nancy gave me sympathetic glances when the last bell rang. Everyone stood up to leave except me.

Ms. Holland sat at Ms. Colman's desk, straightening her books.

"I am afraid I will miss the school bus," I said in a small voice.

"I am sure it will wait for you," said Ms. Holland. "And this will not take long." She stood up and faced me. "Karen, I am extremely disappointed in you. I was told by Ms. Colman that all of the children in her class were well behaved, hardworking, courteous, and honest. But you played with a toy during class time and then complained after I took it away from you. And now this. Taking it from Ms. Colman's desk! I do not know what to do or say to you."

I hung my head and waited for her to go on. I suspected that, even though she said she did not know what to say to me, she would come up with something.

Well, I had something to say to her too. I was just waiting for the chance to say it.

"Do you have anything to say for yourself?" asked Ms. Holland.

This was my chance, so I took it.

"As a matter of fact, I do," I said. "The Genius is my yo-yo. I paid for it myself with my own money that I saved. I brought it to school and played with it on the playground. We are allowed to play with toys on the playground. I took it out in class to show Hannie and Hank how a pendulum works. I was not playing with it at all. You

can ask Hannie and Hank if you do not believe me. But you did not listen to me and took my yo-yo anyway. That was not fair. Then, the next day, when I asked for it back, you did not give it to me even though the class rule said you should. You can ask anyone in the class about that rule. So you took my yo-yo from me for no reason and then broke Ms. Colman's class rule. I should not be punished for taking something back that should not have been taken from me in the first place and then should have been returned."

I took a deep breath and crossed my arms in front of my chest. So there, I added silently to myself.

I glared at Ms. Holland. She looked back at me. Her eyes were wide and her mouth was hanging open a little bit. I braced myself for her to start yelling.

"Karen," Ms. Holland said quietly, at long last. "What you said about not playing with your yo-yo in class may be true. And it also may be true that Ms. Colman has a rule about returning toys after one day. The fact remains, however, that I took your yo-yo from you because I thought you were playing with it. And as I told you earlier when you asked that your yo-yo be returned, when I am the teacher, I set the rules for the classroom. You do remember my saying that, don't you?"

I nodded. "Yes."

"Now, you broke my class rule by returning the yo-yo to yourself," said Ms. Holland. "But more important, you broke a rule of ethics. Do you know what ethics are?"

"Is that like the difference between right and wrong?" I asked.

"Correct," said Ms. Holland. "You broke a rule of ethics — you did the wrong thing — by going into Ms. Colman's desk and stealing something out of it. That action was wrong, no matter how strongly you felt the yo-yo should be returned to you. You can see that, I hope?"

"Well, yes, I guess so," I said grudgingly.

"I am glad you see that," said Ms. Holland. "Now, I can tell that you are a very bright girl who believes in standing up for herself. I believe in standing up for myself too, and maybe that is why we have butted heads about this. What do you say we call a truce? I will not tell the principal or your parents that you took something out of Ms. Colman's desk, because now I understand a little bit more about why you did it. And you will agree to abide by my class rule, and resign yourself to the idea that you will not get your yo-yo back until next week, when Ms. Colman returns, because now you understand that taking the yo-yo back was wrong. Fair?"

I thought about it for a few moments. It seemed like we were both saying we had been a little wrong and a little right. I still hated the fact that I would not have the Genius again until next week, but I was glad Ms. Holland would not tell my parents or the principal about this. And I had to admit, I had known deep down that I should not have taken the Genius. It seemed fair enough.

"Fair," I said, and we shook on it.

Sigh. I was not a happy second-grader that afternoon. The first thing I saw when I walked through the door at home was Andrew playing with his yo-yo.

"Look, Karen!" he cried when he saw me. "Watch what I can do."

He flipped his yo-yo out in a big circle, did some sort of twist thing with his wrist that made his yo-yo hop in a funny way, and caught it. And he is only four going on five.

"That is great, Andrew," I said sadly.

I went straight to my room without stopping for a snack. I wanted to be alone.

My four-year-old brother can do yo-yo tricks that I cannot, I said to myself. And since Ms. Holland had the Genius again, I could not practice with it.

Sigh.

The phone rang, and I heard Kristy call my name.

"Coming," I said.

I went out to the hall and picked up the phone. "Hello?"

"Hi, Karen," said Hannie.

"Hi," I said sadly.

"That was so, so mean of Ms. Holland today," said Hannie. "Taking your yo-yo from you for the second time, when the class rule says she has to give it back to you. Why did she do that?"

Hannie still did not know that I had stolen the Genius out of Ms. Colman's desk. And I still did not want to tell her.

"Oh, I do not know," I said vaguely. "I am sure she had some reason or other."

"Well, I think it is terrible," said Hannie. "Terrible and unfair. And you are being so brave about it."

"Thank you," I said modestly.

"Why, someone should do something about this," Hannie went on. "We cannot let

Ms. Holland get away with being so mean to our class."

"That is nice of you to say," I said. "But I do not think there is anything we can do. I will have to wait till Ms. Colman gets back."

"Hmm," said Hannie. "Maybe so. Anyway, I just thought of something. I have to call Nancy. I will talk to you later, okay, Karen?"

"Okay," I said. " 'Bye, Hannie."

" 'Bye."

Pop Quiz

I was hoping that since we had agreed on a truce, all my troubles with Ms. Holland were behind me.

How wrong I was.

"Put away your books and take out a clean sheet of paper and a pencil," Ms. Holland said as we took our seats on Thursday morning. "We are going to have a pop quiz on our spelling homework."

"Ugh!" A groan went around the classroom. (I did not groan. First, because I did not want to make Ms. Holland mad at me

63

again. And second, because I am an excellent speller.)

Ms. Colman never gives pop quizzes. I have heard Kristy talk about having them in middle school. But second-graders just do not have them.

"Quiet, please," said Ms. Holland. "The first word is *thread*."

Ms. Holland read out ten words, and we had to spell them. (I was sure I spelled them all correctly. As I said, I am an excellent speller. I was even a spelling-bee champion once.)

After the pop quiz was over, we handed in our papers. Ms. Holland told us to read at our desks quietly while she graded them.

I could hear her red pencil go *scritch, scritch* on the papers as she marked them.

Suddenly Ms. Holland's pencil went *snap*.

I looked up from my book. (I was reading *Ramona the Pest* by Beverly Cleary. I had read it before, but when you really love a book, you do not mind reading it twice.)

Ms. Holland looked at her pencil. The

tip was broken. She reached into the desk drawer. I was not sure whether she was reaching for a new pencil or for a sharpener.

Then a very, very odd thing happened. Ms. Holland gasped and quickly closed the desk drawer. She had neither a new pencil nor a sharpener.

Ms. Holland looked up. She looked right at me. Her face was turning red fast.

"Karen, may I see you in the hallway, please?" she asked.

"Okay," I said. I wondered if she wanted me to run an errand for her.

We walked out of the classroom. She closed the door behind us.

Then Ms. Holland did another odd thing. She knelt down so that her face was level with mine.

And she said very calmly, "Karen, I want you to tell me the truth. What did you do with your yo-yo?"

My eyes opened wide. "The Genius is missing?"

Suspects, Suspects

Well, if you think Ms. Holland was mad at me the first time the yo-yo disappeared, you should have seen her the second time. She was furious.

I swore that I had not taken it. She asked me again. I swore again. I could tell that she did not really believe me, but there was nothing she could do. She had no proof.

I was very upset, not only because Ms. Holland was accusing me unfairly, but because my beloved yo-yo had been stolen! It would take me months to save up enough money to replace it.

That afternoon Hannie and Nancy came over to the big house to play.

"We are so, so sorry that you got in trouble today," said Hannie.

Ms. Holland had announced to the class that someone had stolen my yo-yo out of Ms. Colman's desk. She had looked at me the whole time she was talking. It was as if she were holding up a sign that said, *I think Karen Brewer stole her own yo-yo out of Ms. Colman's desk.* I had told Hannie and Nancy that Ms. Holland thought I was the thief. And I had finally admitted to them that I had taken it the first time.

"Yes," said Nancy. "So sorry. We really are."

"It is okay," I said. "I know I did not do it. And it is not your fault. You do not need to be sorry."

Hannie and Nancy looked at each other.

"We are sorry anyway," said Hannie. "We

did not know you had already swiped it out of Ms. Colman's desk once before."

"It is okay, really," I said, smiling. "There was nothing you could have done to change what happened."

Hannie and Nancy looked at each other again. They really seemed to know how I felt.

"What great friends I have," I said, hugging them. "Three cheers for the Three Musketeers!"

"Hip, hip, hooray!" we cheered. Hannie and Nancy did not cheer as loudly as I did.

At school the next day, I could tell that Ms. Holland was still watching me closely. That was okay. She would find out I was innocent. And in the meantime, I was watching my classmates closely. One of them had the Genius, and I was going to find out who. I wanted my yo-yo back, and I wanted to clear my name.

On the playground after lunch, Pamela

came skipping up to me, flipping her yo-yo up and down.

"Where is your yo-yo, Karen?" she asked. "Oh, I forgot," she went on in a fakey voice. "You cannot play with it now, because Ms. Holland would catch you with it. You will just have to wait until later to play with your stolen toy, I guess."

Grrr. My eyes narrowed behind my pink glasses.

"You do not know what you are talking about, Pamela Harding," I said.

"I know enough to know that you are a teacher's-desk-opening yo-yo snatcher," said Pamela, "and that you are lying about it and trying to get everyone in trouble for what you did."

I bunched up my face. "Stop it," I said. "I did not take it, and I am not lying, and someone *else* took it, and if that person gets in trouble for it, fine, because they should, and they had better give me back my yo-yo too, or else!"

"Or else what?" snarled Pamela.

"Children!" said Ms. Holland, striding toward us. "Break it up. No bickering on the playground."

Pamela turned and flounced off in one direction, and I stalked off in the other.

I sat down on the edge of the blacktop. I was trying not to cry. I almost wished I had never brought the Genius to school in the first place. All of my friends could do tons of cool tricks, and I could not even practice. What an awful week! And now someone had stolen my yo-yo and was probably playing with it in secret.

Who would steal my yo-yo out of Ms. Colman's desk? And why? In my head I made a list of possible suspects and their reasons for taking the Genius:

- Pamela Harding — because it is exactly the kind of meanie-mo thing she would do
- Bobby Giannelli — because the Genius is a better yo-yo than his

- Tammy Barkan — because her twin sister, Terri, has a yo-yo and she does not

Pretty soon just about everyone in my class was on the list of suspects, except Hannie and Nancy. I knew they would never have done such a thing.

But everyone else could have. It was very confusing.

Only one thing was clear: I needed my yo-yo back.

Sadderday and No-funday

That weekend was terrible. Saturday was Sadderday, and Sunday was No-funday.

Andrew spent all day Sadderday — I mean, Saturday — practicing with his yo-yo. He learned two new tricks. I could not stand it! My little brother knew way more tricks than I did.

I was miserable, and there was nothing I could do about it. I did not want my whole big-house family to know about my yo-yo disaster, so I pretended I was practicing in my room.

About the only nice thing that happened was that on No-funday — I mean, Sunday — afternoon Hannie and Nancy came over for a visit.

They rang the front doorbell and I ran to answer it.

Hannie was holding a plateful of cookies.

"My mom and I made these for you," said Hannie. She handed me the plate. "Chocolate-peanut-butter chip."

"Thank you!" I said, surprised.

"And I made you some special bookmarks," said Nancy. She held out four bookmarks. One was red, one was green, one was blue, and one was purple. "They have glitter on them," she added.

"I see that," I said. "They are beautiful. Come inside, and we can eat cookies and look at the bookmarks."

We went to the kitchen. For once, we had the kitchen to ourselves. There are a lot of rooms in the big house, but there are also a lot of people. Sometimes it is hard to find privacy.

"These bookmarks are perfect," I said, munching on a cookie. "Since I do not have the Genius to play with, I have been reading a lot. Now I will never lose my place again."

"We are glad you like your presents," said Hannie.

Nancy nodded.

"You guys are the best," I said, picking up another cookie. I smiled at them. "I would be lost without the other two Musketeers. Listen — can you help me solve this problem? I have been thinking and thinking about it, but I cannot crack the case. Who could have taken my yo-yo out of Ms. Colman's desk? Who had *motive* and *opportunity*?" (Motive and opportunity are the things every good detective looks for in a crime. I have solved several mysteries before, and I know all about motive and opportunity. Motive means a good reason. And opportunity means a good chance to commit the crime.)

"Well . . . it could have been almost

anyone," said Hannie, tapping her fingers against the table.

"Maybe someone you least suspect," added Nancy.

"Oh, I suspect everyone!" I said.

"You do?" said Hannie. She and Nancy looked at each other.

"Of course," I said. "No one is innocent until proven not guilty, that is my motto. I mean, except you guys, of course. Here, I will show you my list of suspects."

I ran to my room, fetched a sheet of paper from my desk, and returned to the kitchen. On the paper were written the names of everyone in Ms. Colman's class (except for Hannie and Nancy). Hannie and Nancy read the suspect list.

"This is a good list," said Hannie. "It could be anyone."

"Though it is possible that the person who took your yo-yo is not on that list," said Nancy.

"How could that be?" I took the list back and read it carefully. "That is everyone in the class, except you guys. Do you think it could be one of the other teachers? Or one of the cafeteria workers? Or Ms. Holland herself? Hmm," I said thoughtfully. "Maybe so. Even grown-ups could appreciate how great a yo-yo the Genius is."

I wrote down the names of some of the school workers.

"You guys are a huge help," I said, popping one last cookie into my mouth. "Thanks to you, I am sure I will find the culprit sooner or later."

Ms. Colman Returns

Hooray! On Monday Ms. Colman was back in school. Our class gave a loud cheer when we saw her. (We love Ms. Colman.)

But before class started, Ms. Colman asked me to go out into the hallway with her. She wanted to speak to me in private. At last, I thought. A chance to set the record straight.

"Ms. Holland told me what happened last week," Ms. Colman said.

"How much did she tell you?" I asked meekly. I remembered that Ms. Holland and

I had made a deal that she would not tell Ms. Colman that I had swiped the Genius out of Ms. Colman's desk. But since Ms. Holland suspected that I had done it again, maybe the deal was off.

"She did not go into specifics," said Ms. Colman. "She merely said that you and she had some run-ins early in the week. And that later in the week someone took your yo-yo, which she had taken from you, out of my desk. Is this true?"

"Yes," I said. "And I was not the one who took the yo-yo on Thursday." (That was true. I had taken the yo-yo on Tuesday.) "I do not know who has my yo-yo. I am trying to catch the thief."

"Okay, Karen, I believe you," said Ms. Colman. "Now I think we should go back inside."

When I returned to my seat, Ms. Colman spoke to the class.

"Your substitute teacher, Ms. Holland, told me that you were all a joy to work with last week," said Ms. Colman. "However, we had one unpleasant incident, which I hope will be set right. I am asking whoever took Karen's yo-yo out of my desk last Thursday to please return it now. There will be no questions asked, and no punishments."

Ms. Colman waited. Nobody moved.

"Okay," said Ms. Colman. "Perhaps the person would prefer to return it when no one is around. Fine. But I expect to see the yo-yo on my desk before the end of the day."

Everyone started whispering about who the yo-yo thief might be. Several people looked at me.

"Moving on," said Ms. Colman loudly, to regain our attention. "I would like to tell you a little about the conference I attended last week. It was a conference for teachers. We learned about new and exciting ideas for making field trips more fun, planning long-term projects, and arranging for special speakers to come and help us with things we do in the classroom. We teachers learned a lot and exchanged ideas. I wish you all could have been there, as I am sure you also would have learned a lot. And you would have had many good ideas too."

Just then a good idea came to me. Ms. Colman was talking about special speakers, and how they relate to things we do in the classroom. Special speakers like . . . the yo-yo professionals from Team Yo!, for instance, who demonstrate science ideas with yo-yos.

I was just starting to raise my hand when Ms. Colman called on Pamela.

"I was thinking," said Pamela.

Do not hurt yourself, I said silently.

"There is a professional yo-yo troupe called Team Yo! that teaches science with yo-yos," Pamela continued. "Maybe they could come to Stoneybrook Academy, as special speakers, and teach our class."

Hey! Pamela was stealing my good idea!

"That is an excellent suggestion, Pamela," said Ms. Colman. "I will consider it."

Grrr. Pamela is *such* a meanie-mo. And it occurred to me — anyone who was willing to steal one of my ideas might be willing to steal my yo-yo too. I smelled a rat, and her name was Pamela.

Den of Thieves

"Who took my crayons?" Natalie Springer asked, pulling up her socks. We were returning to our classroom after lunch. "I left my crayons in my desk, and now they are gone. The yo-yo thief has struck again!"

Natalie looked at me, as if she thought that I had taken her crayons.

Boo and bullfrogs. Now even Natalie thought I was the yo-yo thief, and Natalie was about the least suspicious person in my whole class.

It had been a long morning for me. First,

Hank Reubens lost a special cool rock that he had found on the playground.

"I left it right here!" he had yelled, pointing at a bare patch in the middle of the soccer field. "It was a shiny white rock with a green line through it. Where did it go?"

"Who knows?" I said. "We have been running through here all recess. Maybe someone kicked it accidentally. You should look around in the grass for it."

"Maybe it was not an accident," Hank said. "Maybe someone took it. Maybe it was the same person who took your yo-yo out of Ms. Colman's desk, *Karen*."

"I do not know what you are talking about," I said, and walked away.

Next Audrey Green could not find her lunch money.

"I am sure I put it in my pocket," she said. "Now I cannot find it. The yo-yo thief must have stolen it."

Audrey glared at me.

"What, right out of your pocket?" I asked. "How would someone do that?"

"I do not know," said Audrey. "You tell me, Karen."

"Maybe now that Karen cannot play with her yo-yo at school," said Pamela, "she has taken up another skill. Pickpocketing!"

"Oh, be quiet, Pamela," I said. "You are too silly for words."

It was ridiculous to think that I — or anyone else — would have picked Audrey's pocket for her lunch money. But I could see some of the other kids did not believe that. They thought I was the yo-yo thief.

And now even Natalie was accusing me.

It was not fair. I was not the yo-yo thief! In fact, I was the only one who had been a real victim of the thief, whoever he or she was. Hank had lost a rock that he had found fifteen minutes before. Audrey had probably not even lost her lunch money — it was most likely in her desk or her schoolbag or something. I was sure it would turn up. The same with Natalie's crayons. People borrow one another's crayons all the time. And anyway, lunch money and crayons were not nearly as valuable as a top-of-the-line yo-yo like the Genius.

"Class," said Ms. Colman, "I have been hearing a lot of talk of stealing. I do not like to think that one of us is a thief. I wonder whether some mistake was made about Karen's yo-yo — that it was not taken from my desk, but somehow lost or misplaced. Ms. Holland would not be the first substitute teacher who made a simple mistake while teaching in an unfamiliar classroom."

My classmates and I nodded doubtfully. Maybe it was true. Maybe there really was no yo-yo thief. But maybe not!

"I am still hoping that if someone did take the yo-yo, that someone will return it to me voluntarily," Ms. Colman went on. "But in the meantime, I have an idea for how we can locate the yo-yo if it is just lost."

Ms. Colman's Plan

On Wednesday morning we put Ms. Colman's plan into action. Her idea was to recreate the morning of the crime. All the kids in my class would do exactly what they had done the morning my yo-yo disappeared from Ms. Colman's desk.

"By reenacting last Thursday morning, we might be able to figure out how the yo-yo was lost, if it was lost," said Ms. Colman. "And if the yo-yo was not lost, maybe the reenactment will convince the person who took the yo-yo to return it to me in private."

All the kids in my class went out to the playground and tried to remember what they had been doing that Thursday morning before school started.

It was easy for me. I had missed the school bus that morning and Nannie had driven me to school. (It was not my fault I missed the bus. Shannon had run off with my gym sneakers, and it had taken awhile to find them.) So during the reenactment, I stood at the edge of the playground and watched the other kids.

Pamela, Leslie, and Jannie gathered near the swing set and practiced yo-yo tricks.

Terri and Tammy Barkan sat on a bench and did their spelling homework from last week. (Terri still could not remember how to spell *believe*.)

Ricky, Hank, Bobby, and Ian Johnson played foursquare, and then went to the water fountain near the school entrance to get a drink of water.

Addie, Sara Ford, and Audrey played freeze tag. (It looked like fun. I wanted to join in, but I remembered that I was not supposed to be at school yet.)

Hannie and Nancy looked at their watches and started to walk into the school.

"Hannie! Nancy!" I called. "Why are you going inside?"

They stopped. "Because, um, this is what we did last Thursday," said Nancy.

"But why?" I asked. All the other kids in my class were playing outside. Only Hannie and Nancy were going in early.

They looked at each other.

"We, um . . . we had to ask the principal a question," said Hannie. "Yes, that is it. I mean, actually, we asked one of the secretaries in the office a question. I forget which one. Which secretary, I mean. So you cannot check. The question was, um, about lunch money. Or something. I forget."

"Right," said Nancy. "That was it exactly. That is what we were doing. 'Bye, Karen!" And she and Hannie rushed inside.

Well, that was pretty strange, I thought. But wait — if they were inside the school at that time, maybe they had seen something. Maybe, without realizing it, they had seen someone coming out of Ms. Colman's class — someone who could have stolen the Genius!

Caught Red-handed!

The reenactment did not work. Everyone did everything they had done before, and nothing turned up. I asked Hannie and Nancy if they had seen anyone in Ms. Colman's room, and Hannie said, "We were not anywhere near Ms. Colman's room!"

"Yeah!" Nancy said. "How could we have seen anyone if we were not anywhere near Ms. Colman's room at all?"

"I was just asking," I said.

In the meantime, I was still going crazy without the Genius. On the bright side, my classmates were no longer quite so suspicious of me. Ms. Colman's plan had convinced them my yo-yo was plain old lost, not stolen. Plus, Natalie found her crayons in her cubby, where she had left them. Hank found a rock on the playground that was even cooler than the one he had lost. And Audrey realized she had left her lunch money on the kitchen counter at home. (Audrey apologized to me for thinking I was a pickpocket.)

So my classmates did not think I was a thief. But I still had no yo-yo.

At recess on Thursday, the day after Ms. Colman's reenactment, I was helping Bobby and Sara learn a new trick with their yo-yos. (Even though I did not have the Genius anymore, I was still trying to keep up with my yo-yoing. I had watched *Mastering the Art of the Yo-Yo* seven more times.) Hannie and Nancy were there too.

"Will you be showing Bobby and Sara this trick for awhile, Karen?" Hannie asked.

"Yes, I guess so," I said. "Why?"

"Oh, no reason," said Nancy. "We have to go now. You stay here. 'Bye."

They ran off. I shook my head. Sometimes I could not figure them out, even though we are the Three Musketeers.

A few minutes later the bell rang, signaling the end of recess. I wondered where the other two Musketeers had gone. I did not see them anywhere on the playground.

Oh well, I said to myself. I guessed I would see Hannie and Nancy in Ms. Colman's room. I filed into the school building with the rest of my class.

When we got to our classroom, I saw something strange.

Ms. Colman was sitting at her desk. And Hannie and Nancy were at the front of the room, their heads hanging, their faces red. They looked totally embarrassed and ashamed. Hannie was holding something in her hands. I could not tell what it was, and I had no idea what was going on.

"Hannie, Nancy," said Ms. Colman in a

stern voice. "I think you two have some-thing to say to Karen."

"To me?" I said.

"Karen . . ." said Hannie.

Nancy sniffled a little.

"This belongs to you," Hannie finished. She opened her hands. And inside them was . . . the Genius!

"We are so sorry!" Nancy wailed, and she and Hannie burst into tears.

A Big Mistake

"It all started," said Hannie that afternoon after school, "when Ms. Holland took your yo-yo from you the second time."

Hannie, Nancy, and I were at the big house. (Nancy's mother had said she could come over.)

"But she took it from me the second time because I had swiped it out of Ms. Colman's desk," I reminded them.

"We know that now," said Nancy. "But at the time, we thought Ms. Holland was just being mean and unfair."

I remembered that I had not told Hannie and Nancy about taking the yo-yo from Ms. Colman's desk because I was embarrassed. Maybe I should have trusted my friends and told them. I promised myself that the next time I did something naughty, I would tell them. (I am bound to do something naughty sometime.)

"We decided to take the Genius back and give it to you," said Hannie. "So on Thursday morning, when you missed the bus, we sneaked into class and took it."

"We did not know that you had already been caught taking the Genius out of Ms. Colman's desk once before," said Nancy. "So we did not know that Ms. Holland would think that you had taken it again."

"If we had known that," said Hannie, "we never would have taken the Genius. We were not trying to get you into trouble. We just wanted to get your yo-yo back for you."

"But once Ms. Holland suspected you," Nancy went on, "we could not give you the yo-yo. That would only have made you look guilty."

"We could not even tell you we had taken it," said Hannie. "We did not want you to have to lie about not knowing who had taken it. Since you were so close to being in big trouble, we figured we had to keep you completely innocent."

"But you felt guilty," I said. "And that is why you came to my house with cookies and bookmarks last weekend, right?"

Hannie and Nancy nodded.

"I hid the Genius under my bed all weekend," said Nancy. "I felt terrible about getting you in trouble. I could hardly sleep."

"But we did not want to get in trouble either, by admitting we took it," said Hannie. "So we waited until Ms. Colman was out of the classroom today, and we sneaked in. We were just opening her desk drawer and putting the yo-yo back when — "

"Ms. Colman walked in," I finished for her. "And caught you red-handed."

Hannie and Nancy nodded again.

"And then the whole class walked in," said Hannie. "Now everyone knows we were the yo-yo thieves."

"I do not think I have ever been so ashamed in all my life," said Nancy. She flushed red just thinking about it.

"I know how you feel," I said. "I have been in trouble like that before. It is so embarrassing."

"It is true, you have," said Nancy at last. And she smiled a little bit.

"Remember when I got in trouble with the phone and could not make calls for a long time?" I said.

Hannie and Nancy nodded. They both smiled. Then all Three Musketeers were giggling together.

Stoneybrook Yo-cademy

I could not be mad at my friends. After all, they were only trying to help me when they swiped the Genius out of Ms. Colman's desk. And Ms. Colman punished them. They would have to stay after school every day for a whole week to help Ms. Colman clean the classroom.

By Friday morning things were pretty much back to normal. I practiced yo-yo tricks all the time — except in the classroom! I had almost caught up to most of my friends. On Friday before school, I did a new trick called Thread the Needle, which I had learned from *Mastering the Art of the Yo-Yo.* No one else could Thread the Needle. I started to teach Hannie and Nancy how to do it.

When class began, Ms. Colman clapped her hands and said she had a special announcement.

I wiggled in my seat. I love Ms. Colman's Surprising Announcements.

"Last week, while I was away at the conference, I learned about exciting ways to connect what we learn in the classroom to what we do outside," said Ms. Colman. "As you know, we have been studying pendulums in the classroom. And many of us have been playing with yo-yos lately. Now, one of our students" — Ms. Colman looked at me and smiled — "noticed that a yo-yo swinging back and forth on the end of its string is, in fact, a pendulum. Then Pamela had an interesting suggestion. And so I decided to invite a very special group to come to our class to demonstrate some basic science concepts."

All the kids started whispering. Who could Ms. Colman be talking about? I held my breath. Could it be — ?

Ms. Colman walked to the classroom door, opened it, and said, "Please give a big Stoneybrook Academy welcome to Team Yo!"

I gasped. In rushed the four yo-yo experts I had seen in downtown Stoneybrook! They were flipping their yo-yos around and doing fancy tricks. One of them even had a yo-yo in each hand! My classmates and I were so excited, we could not believe it. It was like a dream come true.

Team Yo! stayed almost the whole morning, doing tricks and showing how yo-yos can be used as pendulums. They also talked about gravity and centrifugal force. It was interesting — and educational too!

The last part of Team Yo!'s presentation was the best of all. They held a yo-yo con-

test for the kids in my class. We brought out our yo-yos and started flipping furiously. Our school had become Stoneybrook Yo-cademy!

After we had all demonstrated the tricks we could do, the Team Yo! members said they could not decide who was best. So they awarded everyone patches. Mine said TEAM YO! JUNIOR MEMBER. It was so cool! And it would look perfect sewed onto my new jacket. Right then and there, I made up a new yo-yo trick. I called it the Flip Kiss. I spun the Genius down into a sleeper, then pulled it up, and when it came up to my shoulder, I quickly leaned over and kissed it. Then I spun it down and zipped it back up. I was on my way to being a yo-yo champion — now that I had the Genius back.

L. GODWIN

About the Author

ANN M. MARTIN lives in New York City and loves animals, especially cats. She has two cats of her own, Gussie and Woody.

Other books by Ann M. Martin that you might enjoy are *Stage Fright*; *Me and Katie (the Pest)*; and the books in *The Baby-sitters Club* series.

Ann likes ice cream and *I Love Lucy*. And she has her own little sister, whose name is Jane.

Little Sister

Don't miss #120

KAREN'S EASTER PARADE

"All right, Karen," said Mommy, smiling. "I can see that the suspense is killing you. Well, today I got a phone call from my sister Ellen. She and her family will be coming to celebrate Easter with us here in Stoneybrook."

"Yippee!" I shouted, leaping out of my chair. This was a fabulous surprise! I started dancing around the dining room. "Diana is coming! Diana is coming!" I sang.

Diana Wells is my first cousin. She is my age. We are like twins. We had a magical adventure together one summer in Maine. I love Diana!

Mommy and Seth laughed.

"Okay, Karen, settle down," Mommy said. "I have more to say."

"More?" I gasped. I put my hand on my chest.

"Diana will be coming to spend a whole week with us by herself," said Mommy, "before the rest of her family arrives. And she will be here in just two days."

"Two days!" I shrieked. "Two days from now!"

This time Mommy did say, "Indoor voice, Karen." But she said it with a smile on her face.